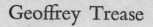

Geoffrey Trease

When the Drums Beat
and other stories

text illustrations by Laszlo Acs

cover illustration by Clark Hutton

Piccolo Pan Books
in association with Heinemann

When the Drums Beat first published 1976,
A Ship to Rome 1972, and *The Chocolate Boy* 1975 by
William Heinemann Ltd
in the Long Ago Children series
First published in this edition 1979 by Pan Books Ltd,
Cavaye Place, London SW10 9PG
in association with William Heinemann Ltd
© Geoffrey Trease 1972, 1975, 1976
ISBN 0 330 25668 8
Set, printed and bound in Great Britain by
Cox & Wyman Ltd., London, Reading and Fakenham

When the Drums Beat and other stories

Geoffrey Trease is well-known as a writer in several fields, having adult novels and non-fiction books to his credit as well as many stories for young people.

Mr Trease has had a lifelong passion for history, and has written many historical novels for the young. He has also travelled widely in Europe and beyond, but his writing comes first and he spends much of his time at his desk.

He lives with his wife in a delightful house on the slopes of the Malvern Hills.

Contents

When the Drums Beat

For
Steven William,
Mary Elizabeth,
and
Philip Geoffrey
Trease

One

The hand that touched Mary in the darkness was so cold that she nearly let out a scream of fright.

In the nick of time she found that it was only her young brother who had crept up behind her.

'Philip!' she said crossly. 'Why aren't you asleep in bed?'

'What about you?'

'The voices woke me.'

'Me too.'

'I hate it when Stephen argues with Father.'

'They're always at it, now,' said Philip in a worried tone.

It was safe to talk, so long as they did not raise their voices above a whisper.

They were kneeling in the little gallery that stuck out, high above the dining-hall. It was dark up there and rather dusty, because it was seldom used. It was still called the minstrels' gallery, for minstrels had played music there in olden days when there was a feast at the long oak tables down below.

There were no minstrels nowadays and no great feasts at Morton Court. Father was always saying that he was only a poor country gentleman and that times were hard.

The children used the gallery as a private place

where they could play on wet days or hide. If they kept their heads down and squinted between the carved wooden pillars, they could see and hear everything that went on in the hall beneath them.

Sometimes they heard interesting things they were not meant to hear.

That was happening tonight.

Their parents had finished supper. They sat in the pale golden circle of candlelight. It gleamed on the top of their father's head as he thrust forward angrily, like Toby the bull when he was teased. It gleamed on the snowy white lace of their mother's collar and cuffs.

At the edge of the candlelight, a restless shadow pacing up and down, Stephen was almost shouting. 'You don't understand, Father! You don't understand!'

And the man's deeper voice answered, just as furious, 'It is you who do not understand, Stephen. You are hot-headed and young.'

'Old people always say that!'

Stephen turned and came back to the table. His heavy boots rang on the stone slabs of the floor. As he drew near the cluster of candles his shadow grew larger and larger on the panels of the wall behind. It was like a huge black bat quivering over his shoulders.

Mother spoke. Her voice was clear but rather shaky. 'I cannot bear it when you two argue like this.'

'And I cannot bear it,' cried Stephen, 'when my own father is false to the King!'

Father jumped up then. His chair scraped back. 'You have no right to say that. I am a Member of Parliament. If King Charles goes against the laws made in Parliament, then King Charles is wrong, and I must stand against him.'

'It's politics again,' Philip whispered in Mary's ear. He sounded bored and disgusted. 'Why must they always go on about King and Parliament?'

'You're too young for me to explain,' she answered. 'But I do wish they wouldn't.' There was fear in her voice.

There had never been all these quarrels until the last few months. Now they happened almost every day, and Mother went about looking miserable. Sometimes there were tears in her eyes.

For several minutes father and son continued to wrangle. The children crouching in the gallery could not understand all the long words they used. Then they heard their brother say:

'But if things go on like this it will come to war.'

And their father cried out: 'God forbid! The King would not be so mad – unless the Queen drives him on. It must not come to civil war. Englishmen have not fought against Englishmen for a hundred and fifty years.'

'Then you and your Parliament friends must do as the King says. Or it *will* come to war. And I tell you, Father, you and I will be on different sides.'

'That is enough.' Mother was on her feet now. 'I will not listen to another word. We have always been a united family. We shall remain so.'

Mary wriggled round and whispered. 'Better get back to our beds. She may come to see if we are asleep.'

Carefully they tiptoed across the creaking boards and groped their way to their rooms. As they parted, she felt she must comfort Philip because he was younger.

'Don't worry,' she murmured. 'It will be all right.'

'Of course it will. I'm glad Mother stopped them.'

'So am I. Goodnight, Phil.'

She lay awake for a long time herself, wondering whether their mother could really make things all right.

Could there be a war in England, with Father and Stephen fighting on opposite sides? It was too terrible to think of.

Two

That must have been the autumn of 1641, Mary remembered afterwards, because she was just coming up to her tenth birthday. Philip was eight. Stephen was fifteen, tall as a man, and he thought himself one when he argued with his father.

Christmas came and went. It was the last happy Christmas the Allen family were to enjoy for a long time.

There was a fine, cold spell. The water of the moat froze inches thick, all round the old manor house. The children raced round it, running and sliding, from the arched bridge that crossed it to the front gate, and so back to the bridge again.

For the first Christmas they could remember they were able to go out without using the bridge. They could open the casement in the parlour and scramble over the window-sill, and drop lightly on to the frozen surface of the moat below. Then, laughing and shouting, they could run off to the meadows.

Only the swans hated the weather. They sulked in the frost-hung bushes, missing the open water where they sailed like ships in their pride. But Stephen took pity on them. He fetched a long heavy pole, and then an axe, and smashed enough of the ice for them.

'And don't *you* go falling in !' he warned his brother and sister.

There was not much snow in the low country round Morton Court. But when they looked out of the upstairs windows, over the treetops of the apple orchard, they could see it lying thick as fur along the high backbone of the Malvern Hills.

Father could not stay to see the New Year in. He had to ride off to London for another meeting of Parliament. With the winter roads in such a state, he must give himself a week for the journey.

They all went into the courtyard to see him off. The sky was red with the December dawn. The horses stamped and blew clouds of steam.

Father bent to kiss them. The plume in his hat shook and tickled Mary's neck. He stood up and looked very straight at Stephen.

'Look after your mother – and everything – while I am away.'

'Yes, Father.'

'I know I can trust you.'

Stephen held the stirrup. Father swung himself into the saddle, gathered his cloak round him, checked the pistols in his holsters. Then he looked round for the two serving men who waited by the arch, mounted and leading two other horses with the baggage.

'Ready, Dick?'

'Ready, Sir William.'

'Then let us go.'

And with a last smile and a wave he clattered under the arch and across the bridge over the moat. In a few moments the little party was lost to sight among the frosty trees.

They had expected him back in a few weeks, but winter ended, and the wild daffodils sprang up in the fields, but Father had to stay in London.

Letters came, and Mother frowned and sighed as she read them.

'Things are difficult in Parliament,' she told the children. 'The King is angry because they will not do what he wants. He has gone away into the North. There is so much to talk over and settle in Parliament, your father says he must take his share. I hope—' she said, and then stopped.

Philip asked: 'What do you hope, Mother?'

'I hope there is not going to be trouble.'

'Trouble?'

'War,' said Stephen in a harsh voice, when his mother did not answer.

'There is no need to bother their young heads – yet,' she said quickly, and she shooed Mary and Philip upstairs. But she went on talking to Stephen in a low, troubled tone.

A week or two later Philip rode his pony over to play with the Gifford boys in the next village. He was back quite soon, and as he ran into the parlour Mary saw that there was blood on his lip.

She wondered if he had fallen, but before she could

ask he crossed the room to where Mother sat checking the household accounts.

'Mother! What is a Roundhead?'

Mother did not look up from her lists and bills. 'Oh,' she said, 'a lot of the men in London and the other big towns keep their hair cut short and wear rather plain clothes. Because of their work, I suppose.'

'But Father wears his hair long—'

'Yes.'

'And he wears splendid clothes! With lace and ribbons and everything!'

'Yes.'

'Then how can he be a Roundhead?'

'Who called him one?'

'Tom Gifford. He said Father was a miserable rebel Roundhead. So I blacked his eye.'

'Philip! You should never have done that!'

'He shouldn't have called Father a Roundhead. He'd no right.'

Stephen had said nothing so far, but his face flamed red. Now he spoke.

'Tom Gifford had every right. Roundhead is a nickname for people who back Parliament against the King. So Father *is* a Roundhead, no matter how long he wears his hair. And just riding a fine horse doesn't make him a Cavalier.'

'The Gifford boys say they're Cavaliers,' said Philip in a puzzled voice.

'I should hope so!' said Stephen gruffly. 'The Cavaliers are those who stay loyal to the King. Everyone round here is a Cavalier. Except Father.'

'Oh, I *wish* he'd come home,' said Mary.

'He's safer among his Roundhead friends in London. This is King's country, thank God. If Father came back just now, he'd be very unpopular.'

Father did come home, early in the summer, but he could spare only a few days before taking the long road back to London. He looked worried and unhappy. The children could only prick up their ears and catch odd scraps of news.

The news was bad. The King was collecting arms and gunpowder and calling on all loyal subjects to support him. Parliament was saying he must obey the laws as other people did. If the King formed an army, Parliament must form one too.

Father said that London and most of the towns were strong for Parliament. But in the country people were more likely to side with the King, especially in the North and the West.

'And we live in the West,' they heard their mother sigh.

'True. Not many people hereabouts think as I do. But a man must act as he thinks right. Even if his oldest friends misunderstand him for it.'

Father went sadly back to London. At the end of the summer he wrote to say that the King had declared open war on Parliament.

Parliament was gathering an army to fight the King. Sadly, Father felt it was his duty to join that army. He was helping to form a cavalry regiment.

Philip thought it rather exciting that Father was now a major.

Stephen cried out that he was ashamed. He would not be able to hold up his head in the neighbourhood.

Mother and Mary said nothing, but they looked at each other unhappily.

Afterwards, they learned how many other families in the country were divided in the same way, brother against brother and father against son.

Three

For a long time there was no sign of the war in their own part of the country.

To Philip's disappointment they never saw a soldier, never heard a shot fired or a drum beating.

Lessons had to be done with the parson in the village. Stephen rode round the estate and saw to things as Father would have done, but he seemed shy of visiting friends in the other big houses. Mother ran the household as usual, but there were no parties now.

Since Philip had fallen out with the Gifford boys, he spent more time at home, nagging Mary to play games with him. Luckily it was a big house, built round three sides of the courtyard. They could lose themselves and make as much noise as they liked without disturbing other people.

There was one dull wet afternoon they never forgot.

Stephen was out somewhere on the estate. Mother was in the kitchen. It was the time when the larder had to be stocked up for the winter, a great time for salting meat and smoking fish, for potting and preserving every kind of food that would keep.

Mary herself should have been in the kitchen, by rights, learning how it was done and seeing how

Mother gave her orders to the servants. But she knew that Philip was lonely and bored, so she agreed to a game of hide-and-seek upstairs.

'Caught you!' she shouted, as she saw him crouched in a shadowy corner.

'Not yet you haven't!' he jeered. And he went racing away, slipping through her fingers like a trout.

Then, turning at the top of the main staircase to go down, he tripped and fell. There was a frightening crash and her heart almost stopped. White-faced, she reached the head of the broad stairs and peered down.

Her young brother sprawled in a heap on the half-landing, where the staircase turned to the right.

'Phil!' she cried, and ran down and knelt beside him.

'I'm all right,' he gasped breathlessly.

He seemed to have broken no bones, but for a moment it looked as though he had broken the wall, or rather the oak panelling that covered it to the height of a man's shoulder. For where he had crashed against it there was a gaping black hole.

'I say,' said Philip, 'Mother will be furious.'

'It can be mended. So long as *you're* not hurt—'

'It doesn't have to be mended.' Philip's tone changed suddenly. He was cheerful now, full of interest. 'There's nothing broken. Look, Mary.' His hands moved over the sections of panelling. 'This part slides back.'

The oblong gap had vanished. She could not tell

where it had been. But Philip loved finding out how
things worked, and already, smoothly and silently,
the panel was moving sideways again. It left an
opening two feet square.

Philip poked his head inside. He called back in a
muffled voice: 'It's quite big. I'm going in.'

'Phil, no – it may not be safe—'

She was too late. As she spoke, the seat of his
breeches vanished and she saw the soles of his shoes
drawn in after it.

'It's all right,' he promised. 'I can stand. And there's
a tiny window.'

She crawled through, forgetting the dust and dirt on her dress. There was just room for them both. A pale streak of daylight slanted through an opening high above their heads.

'It's one of those old hiding-places,' she said. 'They had them in the old King's time, before the Gunpowder Plot.'

'Before Grandfather bought the house. I don't suppose *he* knew it was there. I don't suppose Father and Mother know. If I hadn't fallen against the panelling like that—'

'What's this?' she said.

In the dim light she pointed to a metal spout that stuck out of the wall. Philip explored it with his finger. Then he took out his penknife and pushed it up the spout.

'It's a pipe. It seems to go right up, under the plaster. But what's it *for*—'

'I think I know,' said Mary. She remembered a tale she had once heard about a man hiding for weeks in a place like this.

'What, then?'

'Suppose you were hiding – and you had a friend in the house – he could pour water down the pipe – or wine or even soup, I suppose—'

'And if you put your mouth to the spout—'

'You'd have a cup, silly! You'd catch it in a cup or a bowl or something.'

Philip was not satisfied till they had found the other end of the pipe. As it came down through the wall, it must start from the upper floor. It was quite easy to work out which room, and which side of that room, but it took much longer to discover the secret.

The room was a tiny slit of a room, where nobody had slept for years. There was a broad window-seat, giving a glimpse of the courtyard below. The seat itself lifted on a cunning hinge. Below it was a little funnel, set into the plaster.

'Stay here – and listen!' said Philip.

He raced downstairs. A few moments later she heard his voice, faint and ghostly, coming up the pipe.

'Can you hear me, Mary?'

'Yes.'

Just then she heard something quite different. She pressed her face against the window and peered down into the courtyard. Philip's voice floated up to her again.

'Are you still there, Mary?'

'Yes—'

'Is something the matter?'

'I – I don't know. There're a lot of soldiers riding through the gate.'

Four

So much happened during the rest of that day that the hiding-place got pushed to the back of their minds. Later, when all was quiet again, they talked it over and decided to keep it to themselves for the moment, a secret all of their own.

The captain of the soldiers was talking to Mother in the hall by the time they got downstairs.

'I come in the King's name, Lady Allen,' he said. 'I have orders to search the house for arms and to take any horses for His Majesty's service, as I think fit.'

'My husband is not at home,' Mother said.

'I am well aware of that, madam. And I can guess where he is – but I will not.'

'Search if you like. You will not find much. My son here will show you the stables. I hope you will leave us the horses we need for the work of the place?'

'I shall be reasonable, madam.'

Philip and Mary had to stand with their mother while the Cavalier soldiers opened chests and cupboards and went all over the house. All they could find was a couple of old swords, a pike, a brace of rusty pistols, and a crossbow that had hung on the wall ever since anyone could remember.

They had more luck in the stables. It was sad to see four of the best horses led out to be taken for the King's army.

Something worse was to follow.

Stephen's own mare, Grey Bess, was being saddled. The soldiers were not taking her. Stephen himself appeared again, hatted and cloaked, in his best riding boots, wearing the sword his father had given him for his fifteenth birthday.

'I'm sorry, Mother,' he said. 'King Charles needs men as well as horses.'

She burst out: 'You are not a man—'

He flushed angrily. The Cavalier captain answered for him. 'Younger lads are fighting for us, madam.'

Mary ran forward. She gripped her brother's arm. 'You promised Father! You said you would look after us.'

He shook her off. 'The King comes before everything,' he said stiffly. He turned to his mother again. 'You must see. I have to do what I think is right.'

'That is what your father said!' For the first time in their lives they saw their mother burst into a flood of tears and go running back into the house.

Stephen stared after her, his own face creasing and twitching oddly. Then, without any more goodbyes, he mounted Grey Bess and rode across the bridge. The Cavaliers filed after him, leading the horses they had seized.

In the year that followed, Morton Court was a

sad, quiet house. There were two people now to grieve over, Father with the Parliament army, Stephen with the King's.

Once in a while came a letter, brought by a pedlar or a kind neighbour. It was harder for Father to get a message through. As Stephen had said, this was mainly King's country, and there was not much contact with the areas held by the Roundhead armies.

Stephen could have sent news of himself more easily, but writing letters bored him. He just said he was well and that he loved the excitement, galloping up and down the roads of England with Prince Rupert's cavalry. He had nothing more to tell, so he did not trouble to say it again.

It was difficult to write back. They never knew where he would be. The war rolled to and fro across the kingdom, with fighting in a dozen places at once, and no sign yet of either side winning.

Sometimes Mary, in a black mood, felt afraid that the war would go on for ever – until even Philip was big enough to be a soldier.

Her young brother did not say much about it. She sensed that, in his secret heart, he was afraid. Not afraid of going to battle, but afraid of the time coming when he would have to choose sides.

Cavalier or Roundhead? King or Parliament? Stephen's side or Father's?

She wondered which he would choose. She wondered if he knew himself. It was all too complicated for a boy or girl to understand.

The war came nearer.

There were Roundheads in a city not thirty miles away. The Cavaliers were attacking them, but they held out, hoping that more Roundheads would march from London to save them.

Sometimes a regiment of the King's musketeers marched through the village, their drums beating, their flags streaming in the wind. Sometimes a waggon rumbled by, with barrels of gunpowder and horsemen guarding it. Once the children saw cannons, glinting wickedly in the bright sun.

It was a week after that, when the children had ridden up to the top of the hills, that they actually heard the guns firing far away.

At first they thought it was thunder. But the summer sky was cloudless and blue.

'There's a battle somewhere,' Philip said.

They went slowly along the ridge, peering across the valley at their feet. There were so many woods that they could not see anything clearly. Only, now and then, they saw a puff of dirty smoke or the twinkle of helmets between the trees.

The hills threw back the echo of the cannon-shots. Sometimes they caught the sound of muskets, crackling like twigs on fire.

Then there was silence, and they noticed the birds singing again.

'We'd better go home,' said Mary. 'I'm glad it was not our side of the hills.'

That was the evening their father came back.

Five

He came in the twilight, when they were getting ready for bed.

They all cried out, seeing the bloodstained sash binding up his arm. His face was haggard and grimy with gunpowder.

'Poor old Bella has cast a shoe,' he said, 'but she brought me home, bless her. Be a good lad, Philip – see she is looked after.'

There had been a battle ten miles away. Father's column had run into a much larger force of Cavaliers. He believed that the King's nephew, Prince Rupert, was leading them.

'We had no chance,' said Father grimly. 'They broke us up. Our fellows are scattered for miles through the woods and fields. It was every man for himself at the end. *I* was lucky – I had a safe place to make for.'

Was it so safe, though?

They could trust the servants. Nobody would give Father away. And he was fairly sure that none of the villagers had seen him, for he had come stealthily, using the quiet lanes, and it had been dusk.

'In the morning we can think and plan,' said Mother. She had already brought warm water and was bathing his arm. Luckily it was only a slight

wound, a glancing sword-cut, and Mother was good
at dealing with injuries. 'Just now you must have food
and sleep. You are home. That is what matters.'

Father was still asleep next morning when Walter,
the old shepherd, came limping across the bridge and

asked to speak to the mistress. He gave Mother a knowing look.

'I thought you ought to know, madam. There's soldiers riding this way.'

'Thank you, Walter.'

He touched his hat and hobbled away. Not another word was said.

Mother flew upstairs, the children at her heels. Father was roused. Mary ran off with the bloodstained bandages, to put them on the kitchen fire, while Philip helped his father to slide his wounded arm into his shirt-sleeve. When she returned, he was dressed and ready to go.

But where?

Mother glanced through the window and let out a cry of dismay.

'They're here!'

A troop of horsemen could be seen trotting down the last stretch of road to the gatehouse. They would be on the bridge before Father could get downstairs.

Father spoke lightly, but his face was deathly grim. 'I must swim the moat, then, on the side they can't see.'

'With that arm? And *someone* will see. You'll be hunted down. You haven't a chance.'

'I have less chance if I stay here. They will search the house from top to bottom.'

'*I* can hide you, Father,' said Philip. 'Mary and I found a place.'

He led his father to the turn of the main staircase

and slid back the panel. It was clear from his parents' faces that they had never known it existed.

Mary, with great presence of mind, ran downstairs again. She came back clutching a loaf and a pewter tankard full of ale, snatched from the breakfast-table. She passed them through to her father inside the secret chamber.

'You will be hungry if these men stay long.'

They closed the panel and went down to meet the soldiers, who were already at the door.

To their amazement one of them was Stephen.

His kissed his mother hastily, looking very nervous and excited. 'This is Colonel Audley.'

The officer bowed. 'We have come ahead to warn you, Lady Allen—'

'Warn me, colonel? Warn me of what?'

'His Royal Highness, Prince Rupert, will be here within an hour. He proposes to use your house as his headquarters.'

'It's a great honour, Mother,' said Stephen with an anxious, pleading look.

'The best bedchamber must be made ready for His Royal Highness,' said the colonel. 'There will be six other officers, including myself and your son. There will be thirty soldiers to billet. And there will be hay needed for the horses.'

The next hour was one of wild confusion. The colonel explained, most politely, that the whole house must be searched. So, while Mother and the servants bustled about with armfuls of lavender-scented linen for the beds, washbowls and pitchers of hot water and towels, they kept colliding with soldiers at every turn, flinging open cupboards, testing floorboards, lifting trapdoors, peering up chimneys and even clambering out on to the roof.

Mary and Philip exchanged tense glances. It was lucky they had known about the secret chamber. There was nowhere else where Father would have been safe.

By the time the Prince arrived the house was more or less straight, and Mother had wine and the best glasses set out in the hall.

The children looked with awe at the King's nephew. He was quite young and very dashing and famous for his bravery. They could understand how proud Stephen was to serve as a junior officer under him. He bowed very grandly when Mother made a curtsey to him. He was half German, and it showed a little in his voice.

'I think your husband is not here, Lady Allen? It is perhaps as well. I met his regiment yesterday, I believe, but there was no chance to make his acquaintance.'

The officers burst out laughing. Mary and Philip hated them. Stephen hung his head. Their mother made no answer. Her face was cold and dignified.

'But we will say no more about your husband and his unfortunate opinions,' Prince Rupert went on, taking a glass of wine. 'You have a *son* to be proud of. For his sake, no harm shall come to this house.'

If Morton Court had been a quiet place during the past year or two, it was certainly not so during the next three days.

Messengers were galloping across the bridge at all hours. Trumpets blew and drums tapped whenever the guard turned out to salute His Royal Highness. Loud voices shouted and swore and sang songs late into the night. In the kitchen and the stables the soldiers drank all the ale and cider they could find, and chased the maids who ran giggling and shrieking to escape them.

In the hall the Prince and his officers drank just as deeply, sang almost as noisily, and played cards for handfuls of silver. Stephen did not join in. He was so very junior. He was kept busy running errands and doing all the tiresome duties the older men put upon him.

The children were in two minds about it all. They did not like to see their home taken over by this noisy, rather drunken crowd. On the other hand, it was all very lively and exciting. They would have enjoyed parts of it – if it had not been for Father, crouched in that dark hiding-place behind the panel.

There was never a moment when they dared to open the panel. Night and day a soldier sat on a stool at the top of the staircase, guarding the door of the Prince's room.

Even when His Royal Highness was downstairs, or riding round the district to inspect his regiments, there was a sentry outside his room. There were dispatches and other important papers there, so watch still had to be kept. The sentry had a clear view of the half-landing where the sliding panel was.

It was lucky that Philip had been so determined, that day they discovered the hiding-place, to find out where the pipe in the wall came from.

It was lucky too that, although the house was now so full, there had been no need to use the little room upstairs for one of the officers.

If they were careful, they could still talk to Father, make sure that he was all right, and tell him what was happening.

First, they would make sure that the Prince and his staff were either out of the house or happy at their drinking and gambling in the hall. The minstrels' gallery came in very useful. They could creep into it, peep down, and count the officers.

Then there was only the sentry upstairs to worry about. If he came prowling while they were speaking down the tube, the whole secret might be given away.

Usually, they took it in turns to start a conversation with the soldier and distract his attention while the other one slipped into the little room, closed the door, lifted the window-seat and called softly down to Father.

They found that most soldiers liked children and were glad of a chat to break the boredom of their lonely hours outside the Prince's room. One or two of them were surly or suspicious. Mary and Philip learned to steer clear of these.

On the evening of the third day Mary whispered:

'How is your arm, Father?'

'Not bad, my dear. I shall be glad to change the bandage, but I think it is healing well.'

'Have you any of the bread left?'

He hesitated. 'Oh, yes,' he whispered cheerfully. 'A little.' She guessed from that – he had eaten almost every crumb.

'And the ale?'

'I am only sipping it, to make it last.'

'You need not go thirsty, Father. Listen.'

'Yes, my dear?'

'I will come back in a few minutes. Then you can drink up what you have, and I will pour some more down the pipe.'

Downstairs, she had a better idea. Besides picking up a flagon of ale, she was able to slip into the kitchen and sneak away with a bowl of some broth that was simmering on the fire. She went upstairs again as innocently as she could. Philip had the sentry well occupied, yarning about the battles he had fought in.

'Father?'

'Yes?'

'Hold your tankard under the spout,' Carefully she poured some ale into the funnel and heard it gurgle down the pipe. Then, faintly, she heard her father splutter and spit. She hoped that the sentry would not hear. Philip and he seemed to be laughing and getting on well together.

'All right, Father?'

He chuckled. 'Rather dusty. If you have some more, I will pour this away, and try again.' She poured more ale into the funnel. 'Much better,' he whispered gratefully.

'Drink it up, then. When the tankard is empty, I've some broth to follow.'

'Splendid girl!'

She was tilting the bowl when she heard Stephen asking Philip where she was. As Philip hesitated, the sentry's deep voice answered for him:

'The young lady went through yonder door, sir.'

The last drop of soup slopped into the funnel. 'Someone's coming!' she hissed, and dropped the flap of the window-seat just as Stephen came into the room.

'Oh, *here* you are!' He stopped and sniffed. The savoury smell of the broth still hung in the air. He gave her an odd look and snatched the empty bowl from her hand. He laughed. It was a teasing laugh, an elder brother's laugh, yet at the same time nervous and uneasy. 'So you still go raiding the kitchen, greedy! Aren't you too old now for such tricks?'

She avoided his eyes. 'I was hungry. And the kitchen is always full of your soldiers, so I brought it up here.'

'You did quite right.' He gripped her arm. 'Listen carefully, Mary. *You did quite right.*' Her heart almost stopped with fear. Did he know? And, if he

knew, would he feel it his duty to interfere?

'Why did you want me?' she asked.

'To tell you we're leaving. We're marching north to link up with the King. By tonight we'll all be miles away.' He pressed her arm again. 'Miles away. The next troops you see may be Roundheads.' He laughed. 'You might even see Father. If you do, give him my love. Say – in spite of everything – I am still his son.'

'I will,' she murmured.

Soon the drum was tapping in the courtyard, the rolls of baggage were being humped downstairs and the Prince's dispatch box, and the horses were stamping restlessly on the cobbles.

His Royal Highness thanked Mother. Mary copied her curtsey and Philip bowed correctly.

Stephen gave his sister a last hug. 'I'm glad you found that place,' he whispered. 'I came upon it years ago. I felt guilty afterwards, because I'd kept it to myself.'

'That's all right,' she said. '*Everything* is all right now.'

He grinned. 'Not quite everything. Bella's cast a shoe. She won't carry anyone far until that's attended to.'

Mary flushed. 'You saw Bella in the stable? What fools we were!'

'Hush! You did very well.'

He swung himself into the saddle and with a wave

of his hand went clattering through the archway after the others.

The drums went tapping along the road, fainter and fainter, until the last sound of the war had faded among the hills.

A Ship to Rome

For **Tamsin Burgess**

One

'That was a lion,' said Lucilla, clutching my arm.

'Don't pinch,' I said crossly. 'What would a lion be doing here?'

I myself had heard that muffled roaring sound, yet it seemed unlikely that there would be a lion on a busy wharf in Alexandria, with hundreds of people milling round, the great city glistening white behind us and the harbour twinkling blue beyond the line of moored ships.

Mother, following with the slave who carried our baggage, called to us to go on. 'This is our ship, Titus. Run along, children – up the gangway!'

'There's a lion in it,' said Lucilla. 'It roared.'

'As if there *could* be a lion—' I began scornfully, when that blood-chilling noise came again from the depths of the vessel. I had my foot on the slanting gangplank, meaning to march boldly up it and show my small sister that a free-born Roman boy does not shrink from imaginary dangers. But at that second roar I hesitated.

The slave, stooping under an immense bundle of our bedding and other possessions, grunted something and Mother laughed. 'He says it's safe in a cage in the hold,' she said. 'They send a lot of wild beasts to Rome from here.'

'You see,' I told Lucilla. 'There's no need to make a fuss.' And I led the way aboard the ship that was to take us home to Italy. Mother always called it 'home', though Lucilla was born in Egypt and I had been too young to remember the voyage there.

A sailor led us to our cabin in the deckhouse – 'at the back', Lucilla called it, meaning 'near the stern'. The cabin itself seemed very small, but Mother said space was precious in a ship and we were lucky to have it. Most of the passengers would sleep on the deck.

'Can I?' I asked.

'No, Titus, I think not. You meet all sorts on board a ship like this. I don't want you catching some disease or—'

'But, Mother—'

'Don't argue, dear. I can't stand any more, just now.'

I was sorry then and kept silent. I knew what Mother had gone through in recent months since Father's death. Father had not left much money. He had been in the government service and the pay was low. So Mother had to get us home as cheaply as she could. There was nothing to keep us in Egypt. We were going to Grandfather's farm in the mountains. When I was grown up, Grandfather would give me the farm to run.

Mother started unpacking. 'You can go out on deck and watch the people,' she said, 'but do be

careful. Titus, don't let Lucilla fall down a hatchway or—'

A burly figure loomed over us. 'Everything to your satisfaction, madam?'

It was the captain. He was a Greek, he sounded as oily as an olive, and I took a dislike to him at once. I knew that he had driven a hard bargain with Mother over our fares.

'So far, thank you, Captain Zonas,' she answered, very much the lady, even though she was kneeling on the cabin floor. 'Of course, it is early to say – yet.'

She spoke firmly. Poor we might be, but Father had been a Roman citizen. That still meant something. In my own bundle lay, clean and neatly folded, my long white woollen toga with its narrow purple band along the seam. Only a free Roman was allowed to wear a toga. It was the proud sign that you were neither a foreigner nor a slave.

Zonas might cheat us, but he would show Mother proper respect. All the same, looking up at that sallow fleshy face with its shifty eyes, small and black as currants, I wished that we had found a pleasanter captain to sail with.

Lucilla and I squeezed past him. 'Nasty man,' she muttered when we reached the open deck. 'I hate him.' It was not often that I agreed with my sister, but I did then.

Two

By this time the deck was crowded with passengers and their belongings – Italians, Greeks, Egyptians, Syrians, and others, dark-skinned and fair, merchants, workmen, slaves, old soldiers, all sorts, and all bound for Rome, the centre of the world, the capital where the great Emperor Claudius ruled.

Soon Zonas appeared again, climbed the ladder to the poop above the cabins, where the steersman had already taken his stand at the helm, and bellowed his orders to the crew. The gangway was pulled up, the mooring-ropes cast off, and the square red sail was spread. It flapped and strained as the warm south wind filled it. The deck shifted under our feet like a living thing. The waterfront buildings seemed to slide away. We were off.

Now, behind us, the great city of Alexandria came fully into view with its old palaces and temples shimmering whitely in the sun and the palm trees raising their feathery green tufts against the marble. Then, when we squirmed our way through the crowds on deck and reached the bows of the ship, we could see the open water stretching beyond the harbour mouth. We were passing close under the famous lighthouse, standing up like a giant at the tip of Pharos Island.

'Look,' I told Lucilla. 'It's one of the Seven Wonders of the World. Sailors can see it from miles away.' I shaded my eyes with my hands and squinted up at that soaring tower. There was a statue of Neptune, the sea-god, on the very top, but it looked as tiny as one of Lucilla's dolls. 'I wonder how high it is,' I said.

'Just over three hundred feet,' came the prompt answer from behind me.

I turned and stared up into the face of a tall, clever-looking youth, dressed in the plain toga of a man.

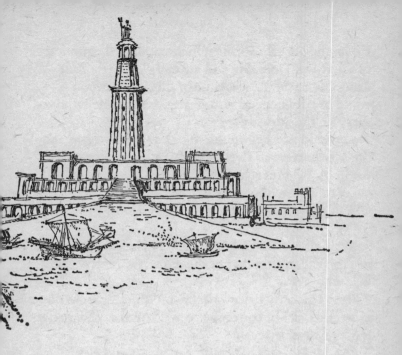

Until you are sixteen you wear one with a single stripe like mine.

His name was Felix and he seemed to know a lot about everything. He had been in Athens and other places, studying to become a lawyer. Later, when Mother got to know him, she told me that this was why he talked so much. A lawyer has to make long speeches in court and ask people questions. It is no good being quiet and shy.

Felix told us about the ship, and how long the voyage should take, and how we should land at

Ostia, the port for Rome which stands at the mouth of the River Tiber. He said we had chosen the best season to travel. At this time of the summer you could usually depend on a steady, favourable wind to carry you northwards.

Our ship was beginning to pitch slightly as she met the Mediterranean swell. Below us, in the depths of the hold, the lion roared again.

'Would you like to see it?' asked Felix.

'Oh, can we?'

'Why not?'

We helped Lucilla down the steep ladder. She was not too eager, I think, but she did not want to be left behind.

It was gloomy below-decks, and smelly. Sacks of corn and bales of cotton were piled high with narrow passageways between.

'And if I know that crafty captain,' said Felix, 'there are a few nice lengths of silk hidden in this cotton.'

'Why hidden?'

'Because when he lands his cargo, he will have to pay customs duty on its value. Silk is more expensive than cotton. Zonas isn't the man to pay more than he has to.'

Suddenly we saw the lion. Its eyes blazed at us in the shadows. Lucilla's fingers tightened on mine.

'He's a beauty,' said Felix.

And he was. A Barbary lion, said Felix, bigger than the Arabian kind, tawny gold, with a mane like a hairy waterfall. He lay with a great bone between his fore-paws, then he rose and stood watching us.

Felix reckoned he must be every inch of ten feet long from the tip of his noble nose to the tuft at the end of his tail.

It was sad to see him shut up in that narrow cage. A beast like that was made to roam the hills and forests. I did not want to stand there any longer, gaping at him.

'Shall we go back?' I said. And I did not mind if Felix thought I was frightened. But he only smiled and said, 'Yes, it must be about time for our own dinner.'

Most people had brought their own food for the voyage, but we were not as poor as all that, and Mother had agreed with Zonas that he should provide proper meals. The deck-passengers were allowed no fires – it would have been far too risky in a ship – but in the shelter of the stern there was a little charcoal stove, with slabs of stone to protect the planks. A fat old slave cooked for Zonas and the few cabin-passengers like ourselves.

We were waited on by a Greek boy named Leontius. He was about thirteen and very good-looking, with fine features and a crop of wild golden hair – but his looks were misleading, for he was really quite muscular and tough, not girlish at all.

I began by not liking him. He thrust our plates at us in a sulky way as though he hated us. But when I saw Zonas box his ears, I was sorry for him. I noticed that he did not cry out, though Zonas must have hurt him.

The captain came rolling back to us.

'You must excuse the boy,' he told Mother. 'I am training him. He hasn't much idea.'

'Don't be angry with him on our account,' Mother said. 'He looks unhappy. Where does he come from?'

Zonas shrugged his massive shoulders. 'Crete, madam. I fancy he belongs to the mountains. He lost his parents in some trouble there.'

'And now he is your cabin-boy?'

'Only for this trip, madam. That's by way of breaking him in.' He spoke as though Leontius were a colt. 'I'm a poor man, madam. Ship-life is rough. I can't afford a cabin-boy who looks like a god.'

'You'll sell him in Rome?' asked Felix. His words reminded me – Leontius was not a boy like me, but a slave. He had fallen into the clutches of Zonas and now he was just like that caged lion below, a thing to sell.

'I'd be a fool not to,' said Zonas, 'a pretty boy like that. Imagine, some rich lady in a vast villa, who wants a page to fetch and carry for her! They'll pay anything, some of these women.'

Leontius came back with the wine jar. He walked proudly. Again I thought of the lion. If that beast ought by nature to be ranging wild in Africa, then

surely this boy should be striding the high pastures
of Crete with his flock.

I had always taken it for granted that some people
should be slaves while others were free. Now I

suddenly found myself hating the idea that soon this mountain shepherd would be scuttling hither and thither in a vast Roman mansion at the orders of some empty-headed woman.

'He'll make a handsome page,' said Mother.

'When I've done with him. I'll stand no nonsense. He must learn to obey. And smile. I thought of changing his name,' said Zonas, 'something more elegant – Narcissus, say, or perhaps Hyacinthus, with those tight curls of his.'

I caught the boy's stormy eye. He might not know Latin, but I fancy he understood what Zonas was talking about.

Three

It was not easy to make friends with Leontius.

We learned Greek at school and spoke it in Alexandria, so he understood my words all right, but for some time he could not believe that I was on his side.

Felix teased me. 'You seem to like our cabin-boy.'

'He shouldn't be a slave. It's not fair.'

'Oh, I don't know. Some slaves are better off than free men. They're always sure of their next meal, anyhow. It's what they're fit for, what Nature intended for them.'

'Not Leontius!'

'Well, don't worry about him. He'll go to a good home.'

'He's not a dog,' I said.

Felix laughed and sprawled lazily in the shade of the sail, reading one of his law-books. That was the second day of our voyage.

It was just after this conversation that Lucilla slipped on the deck and hurt herself. It was Leontius who ran across, picked her up, and got her to stop howling. For the first time I saw him smile. Soon he had Lucilla laughing again. Then we talked, and there was no strangeness between us from that moment.

I kept an eye open for Zonas, afraid that he would not like his passengers to make friends with his cabin-boy. I found that he did not mind at all, and as long as Leontius did his work properly he was allowed to talk to me as much as he liked.

'Don't you see,' said Felix mockingly, 'old Zonas wants the lad to pick up good manners, so that he'll be right for a Roman family? You are part of the polishing process. You are helping to turn the uncouth shepherd-lad into the pretty page-boy.'

It made me angry to think that I was doing anything to help Zonas, but I was not going to stop talking to Leontius on that account.

I think it made matters easier between us when Leontius realized that our family was not rich or grand, that we had no father either, and that we were going to live on a farm in the hills, not in some luxurious city home.

His sad face lit up when I told him about Grandfather and his flocks of sheep, and the rows of vines along the mountainside with the ripe grapes dangling from them, and the milk-white oxen with their gentle eyes. I had never seen our farm myself, but Mother had told me all about it.

'You have good land in Italy,' said Leontius. 'In my country it was mostly stones.'

He knew that he would never see that country again. In any case, he had nothing to go back to. His father and brothers had been killed in a fight between two villages, his mother had died in the

snow. He had been taken down to one of the seaports and there, a few months ago, Zonas had bought him as a bargain in the slave market.

'And now he thinks to turn me into a dandified page-boy and give me the name of a flower and sell me at a profit to some silly hag in Rome! He never will, though,' said Leontius fiercely. 'I would sooner die.'

'Perhaps you could escape—' I began.

'Sh!' Leontius glared down at me.

A great oval shadow had fallen on the deck between us. Glancing round, I saw that Zonas was leaning his fat paunch against the rail of the poop above our heads and leering down.

'Well, Master Titus,' he said, 'I see my lad is keeping you amused. But I trust that he is behaving himself and not forgetting his place?'

'Er – I was telling him about Italy, Captain.'

'Good, good. Teach him some Latin words if you can. He will find them useful in his new life.'

I wondered how much Zonas had overheard. After that I was more careful. I did not want to get Leontius into trouble.

Had he any idea of escaping? He had been very quick to stop me when I started to ask. But if he was thinking of making the attempt before he reached Rome, how could he do it?

'I'm tired of looking at nothing but blank sea,' I said to Felix. 'Shan't we see any land until we get to Ostia?'

'Oh, heavens, yes! It's only this first half of the voyage that is rather dull. We shall get a view of Sicily. Then we sail through the narrow straits between Sicily and Italy, and after that – well, it depends how closely Zonas hugs the coast until we reach the mouth of the Tiber.'

'We shan't get a chance to go ashore?'

'We might – at Messina. That's when we pass through the straits. Zonas may have cargo to pick up. And he will probably want to fill up the barrels of drinking water.'

I said no more. The thought went through my head that Messina might give Leontius the chance he wanted. If he could slip ashore in the general bustle of loading and unloading, Zonas would scarcely delay his voyage to chase him. I should miss Leontius if he disappeared, but I would far rather think of him as happy and free.

Unfortunately, I was not the only person to have that idea.

The next morning we woke up to see the mountainous skyline of Sicily in the distance and a strange dark cloud which Felix said was the smoke over the volcano of Etna. But Lucilla, tugging my arm and chattering at my side, was not interested in volcanoes.

'Isn't Zonas *horrible*?' she said. 'He's chained up Leontius like an animal. And he's going to keep him like that until we're past Messina.'

Four

Leontius was imprisoned in the hold, with fetters round his ankles as well as handcuffs on his wrists. His place at dinnertime was taken by an ugly old sailor who hobbled round with the dishes and slapped down the food in front of us.

Zonas apologized with a grin. 'I am sorry that our handsome youth is not available. I can see I shall have to take care if I am to get him safely to market.' Nobody said a word. 'It is a nuisance,' Zonas went on. 'Handcuffs rub the skin and leave raw marks. He

needs to be in perfect condition to fetch the best price.'

'Beast,' I muttered.

'You said something, Master Titus?'

'I said, "like a beast", captain. Like an animal a farmer takes to market.'

'That's it, exactly.'

After the meal Lucilla and I went below to sympathize with Leontius. He was huddled sadly in the half-light.

'It's not fair,' said Lucilla. 'He needn't have chained you up till we got to Messina.'

'He's afraid I might jump overboard and swim for the shore,' Leontius explained. 'I would, too!'

'We're a good mile from the land,' I said. 'Can you swim that far?'

'Just give me the chance!'

I wished that we could. But I didn't see then how to do it.

Meanwhile the land was closing in upon us on both sides. On our left stretched the great island of Sicily, and now, on our right, rose the coast of Italy itself, gold and green in the sunshine.

'We come to the narrowest part just after we leave Messina,' said Felix. 'The straits there are barely two miles across.'

Lucilla looked at me and I gave her a warning glance. I knew what was in her mind. Later, when Felix had strolled along the deck to talk to Mother, Lucilla came and whispered in my ear.

'If Zonas unlocks his chains before we go through that narrow part—'

'He won't,' I told her gloomily. 'Zonas is no fool. He's been watching Leontius, and he's taking no chances.'

'Oh, if only we could get the key!'

'What a hope!' I said. 'Anyhow, Zonas would spot him before he could jump over the side.'

'You never know,' she said stubbornly. There is no one so stubborn as my young sister.

We reached Messina in the noonday heat. The dockers were lying about, dozing in the shade of the warehouses, but Zonas went bouncing ashore and stirred them up.

'Time is money,' he bellowed. 'Get busy! And where is the customs officer?'

Time *was* money to Zonas, I realized. The sooner we reached Ostia, the more profit he would make. He would save on the crew's wages, he would save on the meals he had to provide for us. Even half a day off our sailing-time meant more money in his pocket.

'We shall leave after supper,' he warned us when we went down the gangway to explore the town.

Felix raised his eyebrows. 'In the dark, captain? Aren't the straits dangerous? What about the rocks – and the whirlpools?'

Zonas laughed. 'I know the straits, sir – been through them a score of times. And you're forgetting – it won't be dark; there's a full moon. Can't hang about here till tomorrow morning, time's valuable.'

We took a walk round Messina but we were careful not to be late for supper. It was Zonas himself who came lurching up the gangway long after everyone else was aboard. He was in high good humour. He had chivvied the dock slaves over the unloading, cheated some fresh passengers over their fares, fooled the customs officers by lying about his cargo, and drunk rather too much red Sicilian wine to celebrate his own cleverness.

'I hope he is not going to take over the helm himself,' murmured Felix. 'This is a tricky coast. We don't want to be shipwrecked.'

But Zonas was no fool. He kept wakeful enough until we had cleared the harbour. Then he handed over the tiller to one of the sailors and retired to his cabin.

'Come, children,' said Mother with a yawn. And we too trailed off to our little cubbyhole. It seemed stuffier than ever, for the ship had been lying still since midday, with the sun beating down on the wooden deck just over our heads.

Mother fell asleep almost at once. I was hot and restless. I felt somehow that Lucilla, though she made no sound, was tense and wide awake. She must have been listening until she could be sure from Mother's breathing that she was fast asleep. Then I felt her warm breath in my ear as she whispered very low.

'What is it?' I murmured back.

'Sh!'

She poked something hard into my ribs. My hand

moved to defend myself and my fingers closed on a large iron key.

'You young *monkey*!' I gasped. I did not know whether to approve or disapprove.

'Come outside.'

As the boy in the family I was, of course, lying across the doorway to protect my mother and sister from intruders. I knew that if I didn't do as Lucilla said she would only scramble over me, and put her foot on my stomach or her fingers in my eye. Most likely both. It was better not to argue.

So I pushed back my blanket, stepped off the mattress, and crept barefoot into the little passage that divided the cabins. Lucilla joined me, and we stood there, two shadowy whispering figures in the half-light filtering in from the moon outside.

'Good girl!' I said admiringly.

I was a little scared at what she had done – and at what we were now going to do. But I saw that we must do it. We had the chance to unlock Leontius from his chains and we must take it. What he did then was his own business. He might not really fancy the long swim, the landing in an unknown country. But we could not deny him the opportunity.

'It was easy,' she said. 'You know Zonas kept the key hung on his belt with all the others? I heard the clatter when he took it off – he was so drunk, he just threw it on his cabin floor – I only had to reach for it through the doorway.'

'Come on, then. The sooner that key is back on his belt, the better for us!'

A ship never sleeps. Apart from the sailors on watch, there are always the deck-passengers shifting and turning. There is nothing unusual about voices whispering or the odd person tiptoeing between the clusters of sprawled bodies and their bundles.

Lucilla and I could pick our way easily. The full moon hung above the masthead like a polished silver mirror. Our shadows were ebony black in front of us. The open hatchway yawned like a pit.

I led the way down the ladder. After the brightness on deck I could not see a thing for the first few moments. The hold was darker, hotter and smellier than ever. The lion growled and my heart bounced inside my breast. But I knew he was safely caged, and Leontius was in the opposite direction. We turned that way and groped towards him.

I think he had fallen asleep, exhausted, huddled at the foot of the post to which he was chained. But, as we reached him, he was instantly on guard.

'Who—'

'It's only us. Titus – and Lucilla.'

'What's the matter?'

'We have the key. She got it from Zonas – he's fast asleep. Drunk.'

My fingers crept over his wrists, searching for the locks.

'Here, Titus!' he muttered impatiently.

'Oh, do be quick!' said Lucilla.

I was as quick as I could be, but I had never unlocked a prisoner's chains before. There was a snap and Leontius had his right hand free. He grabbed the key himself. Click . . . click . . . then a final click as the fetter came off his other ankle. He stood beside us, stretching and rubbing himself.

'How far is the land?'

'Not far—'

'You can see it, plain as plain,' said Lucilla.

'May the gods reward you,' he said huskily.

'But it's dangerous,' I warned him. 'Felix told us. There are currents and whirlpools that could suck you under – and there are always the sharks—'

'I'll risk them,' he said in a grim tone. 'Better die free than live as a slave.' He thrust the key into my hand. 'Can you put that back – before he wakes?'

'Yes—'

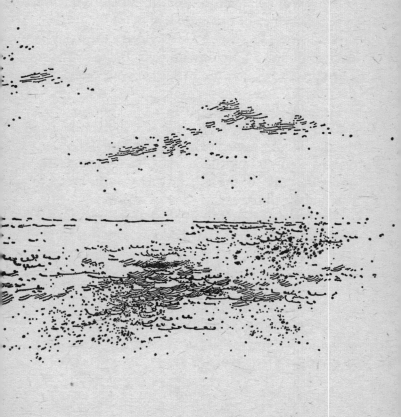

'Then do. Quick. He mustn't know who it was that helped me. Don't tell anybody – even your mother – till you're off this ship. Understand?'

'Yes, Leontius.'

He did not talk like a slave any more. He was a big boy, giving orders to a younger boy and a little girl. I did not mind. We had done what we had come to do and I knew that he was grateful. But there was no time for fancy speeches.

'How will you manage?' Lucilla asked. 'You won't have any money or dry clothes or—'

'One worry at a time!' He sounded almost gay. 'I shall be all right. You must go now. Put the key back. Then pretend you've been asleep in your cabin all the time.'

He gripped my hand, gave Lucilla a hug, and pushed us on our way. We climbed up the ladder and the moonlight seemed brighter than ever. The narrow straits twinkled like glass. To right and left, under the curve of the sail, the rocky shores were pale and dreamlike.

The helmsman must not see us. But that was no great difficulty, for the hatchway was hidden from his view. We reached the deckhouse without meeting anyone or disturbing the sleepy figures curled up in every corner.

Zonas was snoring. We heard him yards away.

'Give me the key,' said Lucilla. Her voice was shaking and I knew that this was the moment when she was most frightened. 'I know just where his belt is lying,' she insisted, 'I can slip it back into its place.'

I had to let her. I would have made more noise, groping on the cabin floor. 'Good girl,' I said, as she backed out of the darkness again. 'And now we must make sure we don't wake Mother.'

'Oh, we *must* see him go!'

'But—'

'We *must*.'

Before I could stop her, my wilful sister was out on deck again. What could I do but follow her?

There was a stretch of main deck behind the deckhouse. The last two or three yards stuck right out over the water. Here, in the centre of the planking, the massive swan's neck of the stern-post came curving up, its gold paint flashing back the moon. Thick as a tree trunk and much taller than a man, the stern-post offered good cover from the steersman on the poop. In any case he ought to be looking the opposite way.

We were just in time to see a figure flit, like some pale moth, towards the stern.

Leontius also was reckoning that the steersman's eyes would be fixed on the channel ahead, and that the best chance of going overboard unnoticed was from the stern rail where it hung like a balcony above the sea.

He vanished behind the stern-post. We sped after him on silent feet. We saw him for an instant steadying himself on the rail. Then he let go, arms spread, hurling himself outwards.

We ran to the rail, clambered on it, leaned out, and peered down. The water was all frothy and glowing with a soft white light as the wavelets clashed together where the ship had passed.

'I can't see him!' cried Lucilla anxiously.

'Quiet!' It might ruin everything if the steersman heard us. I craned over at a dangerous angle, gripping the rail, my eyes scouring the troubled water for Leontius.

Suddenly I saw his head as the dark shadow of the ship glided on, leaving him behind in the moonlight. He was swimming strongly for the Italian shore. His bare arms flashed as they cut through the waves.

'It's all right,' I said, 'I can see him.'

'Where, Titus? *I* can't see him! Where is—'

She never finished her question. Her words tailed off in a shrill scream.

And I screamed too, at the top of my voice. 'Help!' I yelled for all the world to hear. 'She's fallen overboard!'

Five

At once I found Felix at my side. I learned afterwards that he had been sitting in the shadows, enjoying the beauty of the night, and had been watching without showing himself.

'Save her!' I begged.

'It's no good. I – I can't swim that well.' For once Felix was stammering. He grabbed me as I mounted the rail. 'Don't be a little fool! *You* can't do anything. It's suicide for a boy—'

'We must try!' I struggled in his arms, shouting. Some sailors had arrived. They gaped over the stern, but nobody took any action.

'It's all right,' said Felix in a soothing tone. 'Someone *has* gone in. Yes – yes, look, he's got her safely.'

I peered down. I saw two heads close together, one very small, with a draggle of long dark hair like seaweed. It was Lucilla's. And the other was the gleaming gold head of Leontius.

He must have heard the screaming and turned back. He had calmed her frantic struggles and she had given herself meekly to his orders. The ship had swung round – we had been gliding along only slowly in the light breeze – and Leontius reached the

side as a rope ladder skimmed down, and a sailor
dropped nimbly to the water to help him.

In a few moments a dripping, speechless Lucilla
was hauled over the rail and collapsed at my feet,
where I did my best to comfort her. My relief was
soon mixed with dismay, for she was quickly
followed by Leontius – and, to cap everything,

Zonas had been roused from his drunken slumbers and now arrived, cursing and bellowing.

The sailor on the rope ladder had seized Leontius with the best of intentions, thinking naturally that he wanted help to climb aboard again. And when Leontius had tried to break away, the sailor had hung on, recognized him as the slave boy, and held him until a second man could drop to his assistance.

Leontius, already tired by his life-saving efforts, was no match for the two of them. And even if he had managed to break free and strike out for the distant shore, I doubt if he could have escaped now that the alarm had been given. Zonas would have lowered the boat and recaptured him long before he could have reached land.

'It was all your fault,' I told Lucilla furiously when she had recovered from her own ordeal. That remark sent her into floods of tears, and I had to comfort her again. I realized then that no one was as angry with her as she was herself.

All our efforts had gone for nothing. Poor Leontius was back in chains below. And there were a lot of awkward questions in the air.

How had he got free? What were Lucilla and I doing on deck just at that very moment – when we were supposed to be fast asleep in our cabin with Mother?

Neither Zonas nor Mother pressed us too hard with those questions. I fancy they both had their own ideas. Felix, of course, had seen half of what happened and guessed the other half.

'You were a young idiot,' he told me next day. 'Your sister may be excused, but you're old enough to know better. Leontius is a valuable slave, you were robbing Zonas, and by law—'

'Oh, *law*!' I cried. 'All you talk about is law.'

'The laws are the pillars of the Empire,' he said so pompously that I turned away.

Mother asked Zonas if she might buy Leontius. She meant to offer the boy his freedom as a reward for saving Lucilla. If he had nowhere to go when we docked at Ostia, he would be welcome to make his home with us and help on the farm.

That happy scheme came to nothing. As Felix had said, Leontius was valuable. Some rich people would pay almost anything for a good-looking Greek boy like that. Zonas was too mean to knock a penny off the price.

Mother herself was crying when she explained to Lucilla. 'We just haven't that sort of money, darling. We might have borrowed it, if Grandfather agreed to help. But Zonas won't wait. He's sending Leontius to market as soon as we land.'

One thing had made Zonas angry. He could not have Leontius whipped for trying to escape. 'The marks would show on his back,' he grumbled. 'He has to stand naked at the auction, so that the bidders can see he's in good condition. If I gave him the thrashing I'd like to, he'd still be raw.'

'And that would never do, Captain,' said Felix smoothly, keeping a straight face. 'You won't get your price if the goods are damaged. I suppose,' he went on, 'you will tell the customs officer how valuable he is? You'll have to pay a lot of import duty, won't you?'

Zonas winced at the unpleasant reminder. He wore a thoughtful expression as he walked away.

For the last part of the voyage we kept close to the Italian shore and Leontius was given no chances. He was kept fettered night and day except for an hour's exercise to keep him in condition, and, wherever the key was, it was well out of our reach. We won black looks from the sailors if we went near the captive.

One short conversation with him we did manage, when he was brought on deck for fresh air. The man guarding him could not very well forbid us.

'I want to thank you for saving me,' said Lucilla, and her lip trembled. 'Oh, Leontius, I'm so *sorry*—'

'You could not help it.' He looked down at her stonily. 'I could not let you drown.'

'We've done all we can to make up for it,' I assured him. 'Mother's tried to buy you your freedom. She's pleaded with that – that man – but it's no use—'

'And it's no use talking about it now.' His tone was so grim that I could think of nothing more to say. He turned his head and scowled at the coast, so near and yet so far. He did not want our sympathy. Like a sick, unhappy animal he wanted to be left alone.

We felt so miserable and helpless, we did not thrust our unwelcome company upon him again. We longed for the end of the voyage, and we were thankful when at last Felix pointed out the mouth of the Tiber to starboard. The town on the bank, he told us, was Ostia, where we should land and travel on to Rome by road.

Mother began to pack. 'You'd better wear your toga when we go ashore,' she said.

'Oh, Mother—' I began to object. It seemed such a hot day to dress up in a long thing like that.

'Do as I say, Titus. We shall get better treatment if they see at a glance that we are Romans.'

'All right,' I said sulkily.

'I hung it on the rail outside to air it.'

I went off, but although I searched everywhere I could see no sign of it. I reported to Mother.

'Oh dear, that was where I left it.'

'Perhaps it has blown overboard?'

'Been stolen, more likely. This ship!' Mother exclaimed. 'I should have known better. It's not safe to put a thing down – especially on the last morning. There's no time to complain to Zonas – and we can't have a hundred bundles opened when the people are crowding down the gangway. Never mind. Wear a clean tunic and hold your head up.'

Slowly the ship swung round in the river mouth and crept into a vacant berth. The sail came down, the heavy anchors splashed overboard, thick cables

thumped on the wharf and were made fast. The gangway was lowered with a squeak and a clatter. Sharp-eyed officials stood at the bottom to check passengers and baggage before the cargo was taken off.

Felix, with his usual smartness, was the first ashore. 'He has gone to make sure of a carriage,' said Mother, 'to take us to Rome. He's going to share the expense. So there's no need for us to hurry.' And she made us stand back while the other people pushed and jostled to reach the gangway.

When the crowd had thinned, we walked off quietly with a slave carrying our baggage. We had no trouble with the customs men. They could see at a glance that we were respectable Romans. I am afraid it was equally obvious that we were not wealthy and were unlikely to have any valuable goods.

Felix came up. 'I've hired a carriage.'

'Can't we wait and say goodbye to Leontius?' Lucilla pleaded. 'I saw him up there with Zonas, waiting to come off. Mother, we can't just go—'

'All right,' said Mother hastily.

I was the first to spot Leontius coming down the gangway, freed now from his chains, but with a burly sailor in front of him and another at his heels, and Zonas bringing up the rear, watchful for the first sign that he was going to bolt. But it was something else that brought a cry to my lips.

'*My toga!*'

Leontius was draped in a flowing toga, the

purple-bordered toga of a free Roman boy, and I knew in a flash that it was mine.

Felix gasped with mingled amusement and disgust. 'That scoundrel, Zonas! What a nerve!' And as we others stood gaping and mystified, he explained the trick. 'He doesn't want to pay duty on Leontius. So he's pretending he isn't a slave but a passenger.' Felix let out a delighted chuckle. 'But he's gone too far this time, greedy rogue. What a stupid thing to do!' He strode towards the ship and I had almost to run to keep up.

'Felix, what are you going to do?'

'You'll see. There's a famous case in my law-book.'

Leontius and his party had passed the customs officers. The sailors had edged in, one on either side. If he had tried to run for it they would have pounced instantly. Felix went up to them, blocked their path, and greeted Leontius in Latin, loudly enough for everyone to hear – especially the customs men.

'Ah, here you are, dear boy! We're waiting over there, we've a carriage ready.'

The young Greek looked puzzled. Zonas understood. He went purple.

'What's the idea? You can't take this boy – he's mine!'

'What do you mean, "yours"? Your son – or your nephew? You didn't treat him like that on the ship.'

'My slave, as you know perfectly well,' said Zonas roughly. Then, glancing round, he saw that the customs officers were watching us with great interest and he clearly wished he had dropped his voice.

'How can he be a slave?' asked Felix. 'No slave is allowed to wear the toga.'

Zonas began to bluster. The mean little eyes bulged larger with fury. 'What does it matter? The boy was in rags, not fit to be seen. He had to wear something—'

'But a *toga*?'

'This is nonsense! Get out of the way. A ship's captain has more important things to see to. The toga was just a mistake.'

'An expensive mistake – for you, Captain.'

'What do you mean, young man?'

'It was decided long ago in the law courts. No one who had ever worn the toga – even for one moment – could be regarded as a slave. That very act made him free.'

Zonas choked. 'I don't believe it!'

'There was a famous case. A ship's captain tried to cheat the customs by dressing up a slave. It's in my book.' With a smile Felix tapped the round case in which he carried the parchment book he was always studying. 'Read it for yourself. Or let us ask these officers.'

Again Zonas looked round nervously. The customs men were hovering in the background like vultures. His face twitched. I could almost see his mind working. Was it worth while to argue? He must have decided it was better to lose his money and avoid trouble with the law. He would have to pass those officers again on his next visit, and the next.

'All right,' he said thickly. 'You win, you cunning smart young—'

'What language in front of the children!' said Felix.

He took Leontius by the arm and at a muttered order from Zonas the two sailors dropped back. In a dazed tone Leontius asked, as we hustled him away to our waiting carriage:

'I don't understand – where are we going? What are you going to do with me?'

I knew that I could safely speak for Mother when I answered: 'We're going to Rome – and then to Grandfather's farm. And after that you can do as you like, because you're free now.'

'But you will stay with us for ever and ever, won't you?' begged Lucilla. 'Oh, I do hope you will.'

And so far, he has.

The
Chocolate
Boy

For **Liza Burgess**

Author's note This is a tale of England about two hundred and fifty years ago. At that time there was a fashion for black page-boys and footmen, who were brought in as slaves from the West Indies. It was not until 1772, in the reign of King George III, that a judge said it was against the law to keep slaves in England, and they were all declared free. By then there were 14,000 of them, many in London, but not all.

Goose Fair is still held every year in Nottingham and in 1766 there was a famous 'cheese riot', broken up by the Dragoons. Castle Gate is a real street and there are a few elegant old houses left among the shops and offices, like the one Sarah's aunt lived in. And there really are caves and rock cellars cut out below the buildings. St Nicholas's, once called 'the drawing-room church', is still there, near the gateway to the castle.

But surely the name 'Mrs Toplady' is too good to be true? Not at all. It was the name of a leading family in the town. A William Toplady was Tory Mayor in 1682 and an Alderman Francis Toplady helped the Cavaliers to come in and attack the Roundheads. So probably there was at least one real Mrs Toplady who thought as much of herself as Sarah's aunt did.

One

'You are a lucky boy,' they told Sam in the kitchen of the great house in Castle Gate.

'You are a lucky girl,' Mrs Rigby was telling Sarah at that very same moment in the grand drawing-room upstairs.

The two young people had not yet set eyes on each other, but they would have agreed together on one thing. In their own hearts they did not feel that they were quite as lucky as everyone else seemed to think.

'Sam! Stop that drumming, do!' called Mrs Parkins, bending red-faced to lift her cake out of the oven. 'I told you to polish that tray, not give us a concert.'

'Sorry, Mrs Parkins, ma'am,' said Sam humbly. He picked up the cloth again and began to rub the silver tray as hard as he could.

Why was it, he thought, it seemed as though he could never pick anything up without his fingers itching to tap out a rhythm as if it were a drum? Silver trays, wooden tubs, saucepan lids – they all had their different sounds, like voices. If he had six pairs of hands he could have played them all at once, like a band. It would have been wonderful.

But Mrs Parkins, the cook, had no use for his music. Nor had Betty and Jenny, the maids, nor gruff old Thomas, the coachman. They put their hands over their ears or sometimes clouted Sam's. 'He has the devil in his fingers,' said Thomas, 'but then, what else would you expect with a heathen child from foreign parts?'

'He's a lucky boy,' said Mrs Parkins for the tenth time. 'He's in a good Christian home, with a fine mistress to work for—'

'Very fine,' said the maid Betty, who was the sly one, and Jenny giggled, but Mrs Parkins looked severe.

'I will not hear a word said against Mrs Toplady, not in my kitchen,' she told them sternly, and that was for the tenth time too.

In the short time he had been in the house Sam had heard plenty of gossip among the servants, and Mrs Parkins could not check it, however much she tried.

Their mistress was well named Mrs Toplady, for that was exactly what she wished to be in the town of Nottingham. She was a snob from the tip of her long nose to the high heels of her elegant silk slippers. The maids laughed at her behind her back, because she thought herself better than all her neighbours in the tall smart houses of Castle Gate.

'She has fine ways,' Betty would say, 'but she's as mean as muck.'

Mrs Toplady kept the tea and sugar locked up in the drawing-room. Used tea-leaves were good enough for servants, she said, so in the kitchen they

had to drink pale wishy-washy stuff made from what was left in the teapot.

Broken chairs were good enough for servants, said Mrs Toplady. So in the kitchen they managed with rickety old furniture which wobbled and creaked and tilted on the stone-paved floor.

One thing vexed the girls most of all. Mrs Toplady could not bear servants to look smart. 'She's jealous of us because we are young,' said Betty. So, when she or Jenny slipped out into the town for an hour or two, and wanted to make themselves as pretty as possible, they tried to avoid being seen. 'That ribbon is too bright,' their mistress would say. 'Those shoes are not suitable for a young person in your humble way of life.'

But she did not dare to bully Jenny or Betty too much, let alone Mrs Parkins. They were free to leave her and find another place.

Only Sam was completely at her mercy. There was nowhere else for him to go. So he did not feel a very lucky boy.

'Hurry with that tray,' said Mrs Parkins. 'The mistress may ring for her hot chocolate any minute now. And you know what she is like when she is kept waiting.'

Sam did. He rubbed harder than ever. Then he held up the shining circle so that it flashed back the sunshine pouring through the tall sash window over the sink.

'I can see my face in it, Mrs Parkins, ma'am,' he assured her proudly.

It was a dark face, with dazzling white teeth where the broad lips parted in a cheerful grin. The eyes too were merry, as Sam studied his reflection.

They were not always so. There were times when those eyes were full and sad, like the eyes of a lost dog.

Meanwhile, upstairs, Mrs Rigby was telling Sarah what a wonderful aunt she had in Mrs Toplady, and how fortunate she was to be invited to stay with her in this elegant house.

'Yes, ma'am,' said Sarah meekly. But already she was beginning to have her doubts, though it was only a few hours since she had arrived. She was feeling homesick. She was not at all sure that she was going to enjoy three weeks with Aunt Alicia Toplady.

That important personage was looking very smug as she faced her friend, Mrs Rigby, sitting dignified and upright in her silk-covered chair on the other side of the splendid white chimney-piece.

Her dress too was all silk, with a bold bright pattern. She had just had it made for her in London, on her last visit. Mrs Rigby had been wise enough to say how elegant it looked.

'Ah, there is nowhere like London,' said Mrs Toplady. 'But as smaller towns go, Nottingham is well enough. Even Nottingham will be a great treat to poor Sarah, living as she does in the depths of the country.'

'Of course,' said Mrs Rigby.

Sarah did not like being called 'poor'. She thought to herself: if that woman says again that I'm a lucky girl, I think I shall scream.

She bit her lip and vowed to control herself. She had promised her parents that she would behave well. And, if she did not, she would only give her aunt another excuse to say that children brought up in the country had no manners.

'I shall do what I can for her while she is with me,' said Mrs Toplady grandly. 'Her parents live quietly, they know nobody who matters, and they can give the child no advantages.'

'You will make up for that, dear Alicia.'

'I shall try. She seems a dull little thing, a proper country mouse. But I can give her polish, and a glimpse at least of genteel society.'

'She must come to my house and play with George.'

'She will be delighted.'

Sarah felt anything but delighted.

She stole a glance at George Rigby, who sat balancing himself on the edge of the settee, looking bored. He scowled at her behind his mother's back.

The two children had taken a dislike to each other at sight. Sarah had summed up George as a spoilt, namby-pamby boy with a nasty streak in his character. She had seen him try to tread on the cat's tail when nobody was looking. Luckily the cat, as well as herself, *had* been looking, and George's foot had come down on nothing but carpet.

Playing with George was not going to make the holiday any more enjoyable.

'What else did you bring back from town?' asked Mrs Rigby. 'I know you never visit London without learning all the latest fashions.'

Mrs Toplady had been waiting for this question. She broke into a smile of triumph. 'You shall see, my dear,' she said mysteriously. 'Something that is all the rage in town, these days, but I fancy I shall be the very first in Nottingham.'

'What *have* you brought us, Alicia?'

'I'll show you. You will take a cup of hot chocolate, won't you?'

'You are too kind, but—'

'No trouble. Cook will have it ready. George, would you have the goodness to ring the bell?'

Sulkily the boy got to his feet, slouched over to the thick red cord dangling beside the chimney-piece, and gave it a vicious tug. Down in the depths of the house a bell tinkled faintly. George did not sit down again but wandered moodily round the room, fidgeting.

'Sarah, my love,' said Mrs Toplady, 'will you get out the cups from the corner cupboard? My best china,' she explained. 'I never trust the maids with it in the kitchen.'

Glad of something to do, Sarah carried the cups and saucers to a little round table at her aunt's elbow.

She handled them carefully, guessing what would be said if she dropped one.

She had just finished arranging them when the door opened. She heard Mrs Rigby's little gasp of admiration.

'My dear! A real, live black boy!'

Sam marched into the drawing-room, straight as a soldier, in tail-coat of canary yellow, white breeches and white stockings. His buttons shone, his shoes shone, his dark face shone like polished bronze. But nothing shone more brightly than the tray he held aloft in his white-gloved hands, the tray with its silver jug, steaming sweetly with its hot drinking chocolate.

'Oh, in London,' said Mrs Toplady 'all the best families have a black boy to serve the chocolate. It's quite the thing now.'

Mrs Rigby goggled. Mrs Toplady could scarcely hide her triumph. She, first of all the ladies in the town, had a slave boy to wait upon her, just like the grand people in London. Alicia Toplady had scored again.

Sarah thought that Sam cut a splendid figure as he advanced towards his mistress. Then, suddenly, disaster came.

The black boy uttered a desperate, gulping cry and shot forward head first. The tray slipped, the dark liquid sprayed from the falling jug, and Mrs Toplady pulled back her flowing skirts just in time

to save her dress as the chocolate spilled over the carpet in front of her feet.

'You careless ape!' she screamed.

Only Sarah had seen George's foot stretch out, stealthily, and trip the page-boy as he went by.

Two

Sarah's brown eyes opened wide in horror. '*George!*' she began hotly, but her angry cry was lost in the general hubbub.

Her aunt was quacking like an excited goose, and a very wild goose at that. Sam was on his knees, rescuing the silver jug before the last drop of chocolate streamed out, and stammering his apologies. Mrs Rigby had jumped up and was flapping about, exclaiming and getting in the way.

'Ring the bell, Sarah!' shouted Mrs Toplady. 'Don't just stand there!'

Sarah ran and pulled the red cord. Soon Jenny came, and cried out to see the mess. She was sent running for a cloth and pail, and told to ask Cook for fresh chocolate.

'And Betty had better bring it up,' said Mrs Toplady sourly. 'This wretch has done enough damage. When Thomas comes in from the stables he's to give him a good whipping. Tell him that, Jenny. A good whipping.'

'If you say so, ma'am.'

Jenny bundled the black boy out of the room in front of her. George turned to Sarah with a wicked grin.

'So there's a job for all of them,' he whispered. 'Even that lazy old coachman.'

'But it was *your* fault.' Sarah's cheeks burned. She felt tears of fury brimming up. 'If you don't tell my aunt, I shall.'

George's eyes went narrow. 'If you do, you'll pay for it,' he said, still keeping his voice low.

'I don't care. It was a cruel thing to do.'

They looked each other up and down. Sarah's hands twisted nervously. She had been brought up never to tell tales. But in a case like this what was the right thing to do?

George thought more quickly than she did. He must have summed her up as a girl who would do what she said. He put on a bland smile and went up to Mrs Toplady.

'Excuse me, ma'am.'

'Yes, dear?'

'I hope you will not punish the black fellow too severely. By some mischance I think he tripped over my foot.'

'Then he must learn to look where he is going, the clumsy creature. Did he hurt you, George dear?'

'It is nothing, ma'am,' said George with a noble air. 'The pain is wearing off now.'

Sarah was speechless. She could have wrung his fat neck. But she knew it was useless to say anything. Her aunt would never believe that George was to blame.

It was a bad start to her holiday.

She had looked forward so much to this visit. She had never stayed in a busy town.

Five minutes' walk from her aunt's front door brought her to the biggest market-square in the kingdom. Shops and inns stretched along its sides. There was a covered walk with pillars. Even when it rained, she could stroll along in shelter, looking at the beautiful things for sale.

On market-days the vast open space was gay with stalls and crowded with waggons and carriages. She had never seen so many people in her life.

If she walked the other way, up Castle Gate, she came to the castle itself, where the Duke lived, high on a tawny brown cliff. His fine mansion seemed to float above the green treetops.

Below the cliff was a river with a clacking water-mill and a wharf where sailing barges unloaded timber and coal. There was always plenty going on there.

Next to the wharf there were pleasure gardens laid out along the river-bank, with lines of willow trees, shady places to sit, and a lawn like velvet where gentlemen were always playing bowls. This place was called the Spa.

Sarah would have liked the Spa better if she had been free to go there alone, to explore the winding paths and lean over to watch the fish darting in the green water and perhaps make friends with the other children she saw.

Unluckily, the Spa was a favourite place with Mrs

Toplady. She liked to stroll there in the afternoon and especially on Sunday mornings after church. That was when all the best people paraded in their finest clothes, the men in their cocked hats and powdered wigs, the ladies in rustling silk, and the Dragoon officers in their scarlet coats.

Sarah had to walk meekly at her aunt's side. If she wanted to go there at other times Mrs Toplady said she must go with George Rigby.

'He is a suitable friend for you,' she said. 'It is most important that you should have suitable friends. You must not mix with just anybody.'

Sarah did not think George was a suitable friend at all. At their first meeting she had seen that he was unkind and told lies. As she saw more of him, she liked him less and less.

If they went to the Spa, George threw stones at the waterfowl. And if they went into the town he only wanted to show her where the bulls were baited or tell her about a cock-fight he had seen, with all the horrible details of how the birds had killed each other.

'It's a pity there isn't anybody in the stocks,' he said as they crossed the market-place. 'You can throw things at them, and they can't chase you off because their arms and legs are fastened. Those squishy-looking plums on the stall would do splendidly. But eggs are best. You should see the mess, if you land one right in the man's face!' He laughed.

'I think you're horrid,' said Sarah. She was thankful

that there was never anyone sitting in the stocks when they went by.

She avoided going out with George as much as she could, but it was not easy. Mrs Toplady did not ask any other young people to meet her, so it looked like being a lonely holiday. If she slipped away to her bedroom with a book, one of the maids would soon be sent up to fetch her. Either her aunt was taking her out or Master George had called to play.

Sarah grew desperate for other company – and desperate for somewhere to hide from Master George.

One afternoon she had an idea.

Behind the tall house was a sandy yard with the pump, the stables, and various outbuildings. There was one door she had never seen open.

Mrs Toplady had waved a hand towards it proudly, when they looked down from one of the back windows upstairs.

'And that leads to my new ice-house,' she had said. 'Hardly anyone in the town has an ice-house. But they are quite the fashion now. All the great country houses have them.'

Castle Gate was built on sandstone. There were caves underground, which many people had turned into cellars for wine and other stores. But it was Mrs Toplady who had had the notion of making one into an ice-house.

'Next winter,' she had explained to Sarah, 'I shall have blocks of ice brought up here and stored on layers of clean straw until the summer comes.'

'But won't it melt, Aunt Alicia?'

'Not down there under all that rock. The air stays cool even in the hottest weather. And so,' Mrs Toplady had ended smugly, '*I* shall be able to give parties and serve my guests with delicious ices in June – and none of my friends, not even Mrs Rigby who is so rich, will be able to.'

Sarah thought no more about the ice-house until the afternoon when she felt she could not bear another hour of George's company.

She was crossing the yard. She had been to the stables, talking to Bess and Bay, the patient old horses that drew her aunt's coach. She heard the peal of the doorbell through the kitchen window, and guessed that George had arrived. Then she heard Jenny's voice: 'If she's not in her room she's most likely looking at them horses!'

At any moment one of the servants would come out and see her. There was only one place which they would never think of searching.

Quick as a squirrel, Sarah whisked through the low door of the ice-house and slammed it behind her.

And then, as she stood panting in the darkness, she heard the uncanny noise from far below her – the throbbing of drums in the very depths of the earth.

Three

After the September sunshine baking the yard outside, the air within struck as cold as if she had dropped suddenly into a river. Yet there was something more – there was the chill of sheer terror as well – that gripped her for a moment and held her rigid, unable to stir.

What was it, down there? What – or who – was producing these eerie drum-beats?

She remembered what her father always said to calm her fears: 'There's a reason for everything . . .' She tried to be calm as he would have been. She took hold of herself. 'But I – I don't *like* it,' she whispered.

She groped for the latch of the door. If she could have felt it she would have backed out into the sunlit yard, even if it meant an afternoon with George. But in that pitch blackness she could find nothing but flat boards.

Panic began to sweep over her again. Then the ghostly drumming stopped. She took courage. She even crept a pace or two forward. There would be steps down. She must not fall. Sure enough, her out-thrust foot found the edge of the top stair.

Ever so slowly she began to go down. One, two, three . . . Breathlessly she counted. At the third step it did not seem as dark as it had been before.

Five steps down, she could see a flicker of yellow light.

Down went her left foot, then her right, then left again . . . The rock was dry and sandy. The soles of her slippers rasped on it. The steps were roughly made, not all the same size. They turned to the left.

Now she could make out the rock curving over her head like an arch. The dim light shimmered on it. It was pale and clean. There were no cobwebs or bats, at least.

Then the rhythm of the drums came rolling up the tunnel, sending her heart into her mouth. She paused, nearly lost her courage, but the light drew her on.

The narrow passage grew wider. It opened into a round vault. The steps ended in a level floor. In the middle, by the light of a single stub of candle, a small figure could be seen crouching.

It was Sam. His face and hands looked blacker than ever against his white shirt-sleeves. He had an empty little tub between his knees and it was his finger-tips, beating on the hollow wood, that produced the sound.

There were no other drummers, only echoes. The walls of the ice-house and its domed roof flung the sound backwards and forwards. It had been easy to imagine a cave full of people, but there was only Sam.

He looked up and saw her. His teeth flashed, his eyes opened wide and white. He stopped drumming and stood up.

'Missy Sarah?'

'So it was you all the time!'

'I make too much noise?' He sounded scared. 'I thought – down here – I not bother nobody.'

'No, no. You can't hear a sound until you get inside.'

'You not tell Madam? You not complain?'

'Why should I?'

She knew that her aunt would not approve. But

then her aunt would not approve of Sarah's going into the ice-house herself – and certainly not of Sarah's talking to Sam there. Mrs Toplady disapproved of so many things.

In spite of that, she found herself talking to Sam and enjoying it.

Until now, they had scarcely spoken to each other. She had seen him about the house, of course. He carried the heavy pails of water up to the bedrooms. She had seen him cleaning the top windows. She had been nervous for him as he sat on the sill, only his legs inside, leaning dangerously far out and stretching his skinny arms to wipe each corner of the pane. And he was allowed to bring in the chocolate again and the coffee – there had been no more accidents. But beyond a 'Good morning,' or a 'Thank you, Sam,' she had hardly said a word to him.

Mrs Toplady thought that even this much was not necessary.

'You need not thank servants for what they do,' she told Sarah. 'It is only what they are for.'

Sarah's parents had taught her differently. Servants were people. Now she found that Sam was a more interesting person to talk to than George Rigby.

The ice-house was his refuge. Only down here could he escape from his mistress and the other servants, who were always after him for something.

'But don't you find it cold?' She shivered in her muslin dress. 'When you come from such a hot country?'

Sam agreed that it was cold. But it reminded him of a cave he had known as a tiny child in the West Indies. It was so hot there that he had liked running into its cool shade.

'Tell me about your country,' she begged.

Sam told her about the palm-trees and the brightly coloured birds and the warm blue sea.

'Lovely!' she said. 'You must wish you were back there.'

The boy shrugged his shoulders. It was a hard life there for slaves, cutting the sugar-cane. If you let up for a minute, you got the whip. 'A real whipping, Missy Sarah.' He grinned. 'When Thomas here he beat me, he just tickle.'

So, when Sam's master had sold him and sent him to England to be trained as a house servant, everybody had told him he was a lucky boy.

Sarah made a face at that. 'They're always telling me I'm a lucky girl,' she said in a disgusted tone.

Having said that, she felt a little ashamed of herself. Compared with Sam, she *was* lucky. She was free, she was living in her own country, in a week or two she would be going home to her family. Sam was a slave, he had nothing, he would never see his home or family again.

They talked for a few minutes longer. Then he said, 'I must go, Missy Sarah, or Cook she chase me with a broomstick. She call me idlest imp in creation.'

'*I* shall call you,' she said thoughtfully, 'Boy Friday.'

'Missy?' He looked puzzled.

'It's in a book' she explained. 'It's about an island –like the one you came from. There's a man called Robinson Crusoe, and he has a – a friend, a black man who helps him – and he calls him Man Friday. Only you're not a man, so . . .' She stopped and smiled at him in the candlelight.

'I not read,' he said sadly. Then he grinned again. 'I go first, Missy? Then, while they all shout at me, Missy get back in house and no one see?'

'Whatever you say, Sam.'

He took the candle in his dark fingers and lighted her up the stairs. At the door he snuffed the candle and they parted without another word.

Four

At home, Sarah had been brought up to believe that it was wrong to own slaves, but she knew she had better keep her thoughts to herself while she was staying with her aunt.

After that meeting in the ice-house she had other brief conversations with Sam, but she dared not be seen talking to him. She would have liked to be friends, but it was too difficult.

Mrs Toplady always thought of herself as a good

Christian who loved her fellow men. Every Sunday morning she paraded up the street to St Nicholas's. It was not the main church in the town, but it was the one where all the best people went. It was so full of fine ladies and gentlemen and dashing Dragoon officers that people called it 'the drawing-room church'.

The next Sunday she sailed up Castle Gate as usual, important in her huge bonnet, with Sarah at her side.

Sarah was not even allowed to carry her own prayer-book. Sam followed behind, carrying a velvet cushion on which lay their two prayer-books. Just as if (thought Sarah) he were bringing in the chocolate on the tray.

The other servants followed two by two, but it was the black boy all the people stared at. Mrs Toplady enjoyed every moment of it.

When they were settled in their pew, Sam bowed and held out the cushion, and they took their prayer-books. Then he bowed again very humbly, and went to sit with the other servants at the back.

The sermon lasted an hour. As the parson's voice droned on, Sarah's mind wandered. It was just a week now to the town's famous Goose Fair. Her father was coming on the last day and would drive her home the next day.

Her thoughts turned to Sam. Boy Friday could never go home. Even if he ran away, he could never reach his island across the sea. But – could he at least escape from her aunt's bullying?

Sarah began to invent wild schemes. She would gladly have helped him, if only she could have hit upon a way. But the sermon ended without her thinking of any plan that would work.

As they went out of the church, the town-crier stood in the street in his blue coat, ringing his bell.

'Oyez, oyez!' he was calling. 'Take notice that a kitchen-boy, John Wilkins, has run away from the house of his employer. The said boy is thirteen years of age, small and of a brown colouring. A reward of two guineas will be paid to any person giving information—'

Sarah knew then how hopeless it was for Boy Friday. If a white boy could be chased and caught,

what chance would *he* have with his black face? No, she must not tempt him to run away. It would only land him in worse trouble.

She understood now why her mother often said, 'There is a lot of sadness in the world.'

But all sad thoughts were driven out of her head, a week later, when the town began to fill with people for the Goose Fair.

The fair was not only for geese, of course, though she saw hundreds of those waddling up the hill to the market-place in the early morning, driven by farm boys and by country women in straw hats and spotless clean aprons.

There were cattle and sheep to be sold too, and horses and ponies tethered in lines, and farm produce of every kind.

Sarah had never seen such cheeses. They were immense, more like barrels really – or drums. If Boy Friday got near them, she thought to herself, he would want to play on them with those restless fingers of his, but he would not get much music out of solid cheese.

They were so huge that they were sold not by the pound but by the hundredweight. She heard people grumbling in the crowd. 'Thirty shilling a hundredweight! It's a scandal.' It seemed as though cheese was very dear, this year.

That did not worry Sarah. She had no wish to buy cheese. With the little money she had in her purse she wanted to buy gingerbread and some small gifts to take home, ribbons perhaps for her mother or a china ornament, and toys for her brothers and sisters.

Also, she wanted to see the shows. She had heard that there were conjurors and acrobats and performing animals and all kinds of wonders at the Goose Fair.

Only one thing looked like spoiling her fun. 'You must go with George,' said Mrs Toplady. 'A young girl cannot visit the fair alone. Most unsuitable.'

'Oh, Aunt Alicia, why?'

'The fair brings all kinds of rascals into the town,' Mrs Toplady explained with a sniff. 'There are thieves who might snatch your purse and run off with it. Some of these gipsy fortune-tellers might run off with *you*, and you'd never be seen again. But George Rigby will protect you.'

Sarah did not argue. She went with George that afternoon.

George, of course, wanted to go into the tent and see the sheep with two heads. 'Ugh!' said Sarah, and stayed outside. 'It's a trick,' said George crossly when he came out, and she was glad that he had wasted his money.

Gipsies wanted to tell their fortunes or to sell them live hedgehogs and grass snakes. 'I know,' said George, 'let's buy a snake and put it in your aunt's kitchen – it will scare those silly girls out of their wits.'

Sarah thought this would be rather unkind, but she knew that if she said so she would only make

him more set on the idea. She was glad when he said,
'We'll think about it when we go back. I don't
want to carry a snake around in my pocket all the
afternoon.'

They both enjoyed watching the clowns on stilts
and the young dancing girl who juggled with wine
glasses outside her tent. At one time she had a dozen
whirling round in a circle.

'I'd love to make her drop them.' George
whispered. 'I could, too, if I brought my catapult
and hid behind that waggon.'

Sarah hastily moved on through the crowd. Suddenly, above all the hubbub of the fair, her ears caught a familiar sound. She stopped in her tracks.

A drum! And she had heard only one person in the world play a drum like that.

Other people had been struck by that wonderful insistent rhythm. All were turning in the same direction.

George pinched her arm. 'Come on, dreamy! There's something exciting over there.'

The crowd swept her with them. Standing on tiptoe and craning her neck, she saw a striped tent with a raised platform in front of it. There was a red-faced, jolly-looking old showman wearing a fancy waistcoat. And beside him, in his best canary yellow, beating a splendid drum and grinning with sheer bliss, was Boy Friday.

'I say,' George shouted in her ear. 'See who it is? Your aunt's chocolate boy! Just wait till we tell her.'

'But we mustn't, George!'

'Why not? He's no right, mixing with these riffraff at the fair. He ought to be getting on with his work at home. He deserves a good thrashing—'

'If you say a word to my aunt—'

'What will you give me if I don't?'

She did not answer. The drumming rose to a climax and ended with a marvellous roll. The crowd applauded. The old showman bent forward and slapped Boy Friday on the back. 'If I had you working for me,' he cried, 'we'd both make our fortunes.'

The drummer merely grinned shyly, handed back the drumsticks, and slipped away into the crowd.

Sarah led George firmly the other way. They found themselves by the cheese stalls. Here the people seemed to be in a very different mood.

'Thirty shilling!' one woman was screaming. 'It's a disgrace.'

'Who can pay such prices?' a man asked angrily.

The cheese sellers were answering back just as furiously. 'We have to live,' one bellowed. 'If you don't like it, you can lump it.'

This was the sort of thing George enjoyed. 'There's going to be a fight,' he said gleefully.

'Then let's go home,' she begged.

'Not likely, silly baby.'

The crowd was growing thicker every moment. It was soon impossible to move away. Sarah was wedged among burly townsmen, who shook their fists at the cheese sellers and shouted insults at them.

Suddenly there was a rush forward, a wild cheering in front. One of the farmers was wrestling with another man. A stack of the great cheeses had been overturned. There was a roar of laughter. A cry went up:

'Roll 'em down the hill, then!'

The market-place itself was on a slope. The cheese stalls stood on the lower side, and below them a street ran curving down towards the river.

Within a minute or two a full-scale riot had begun. The farmers fought to defend their cheeses

but the crowd was too strong for them. The cheeses were tipped over and, one after another, sent rolling and bumping down the cobbled street.

Then a cry went up: 'Look out, the soldiers!'

Over the bobbing heads in front of her, Sarah saw the helmets of the Dragoons as they charged into the crowd. Swords flashed in the sunshine. Horses reared and stamped, women screamed. There was panic as the rioters fled.

'George,' gasped Sarah. 'We must get out—'

But George had already got out. Without a thought for Sarah, he was already racing down the hill.

She turned to run after him. A man bumped into her and she was sent flying across the cobbles. The fall knocked all the breath out of her and she lay there, terrified. Someone tripped over her. She felt a kick on her leg. Her hands were grazed and bleeding. And the clattering hoofs of the Dragoons came nearer as she struggled to get up.

'Quick, Missy Sarah!'

A warm brown hand clasped one of hers. It was Boy Friday. His other arm was round her shoulders. In another moment she was on her feet again. He pulled her into the shelter of a doorway just as the Dragoons thundered by.

Five

Sarah told her father the whole story when he arrived on the final day of the fair.

'He saved my life,' she said, 'when that dreadful George just ran away. We *must* do something.'

'I will speak to your aunt,' her father promised, 'but I am not very hopeful.' Mrs Toplady was not his favourite sister-in-law and this affair needed all his tact.

He did his best. 'I am very grateful to this black boy of yours,' he said, 'and Sarah has taken a great fancy to him. She thinks he is not very happy in – er – in the town. We wondered if you would let him go home with us.'

Mrs Toplady went mauve in the face. 'I certainly would not. What an idea! Why should I part with my chocolate boy, just because he brought Sarah home from the fair – where he had no business to be, himself, at that time? I never heard of such a thing.'

Sarah's father tried to be patient but it ended with both of them losing their temper. Sarah's father said that it was wicked to keep slaves. Her aunt said he should mind his own business. 'Sam is a lucky boy, and he knows it.'

'Sarah says he's deeply unhappy.'

'Sarah is a pert, ungrateful child.'

Later, Sarah met Sam on the stairs and whispered that they had done their best but it was no use. 'I wish you could run away,' she said fiercely. 'But if you came to our house we couldn't keep you. She would make us give you back. Father says it's the law.'

'I shall not stay here, Missy Sarah.'

'Don't do anything foolish.'

'I know what I shall do,' he said. Mrs Toplady was calling for him in her shrill voice, and he had to hurry downstairs to her.

That evening, when Mrs Toplady rang for her chocolate, it was brought in by Jenny, looking pink and flustered.

'Where is Sam?' her mistress demanded.

'Beg pardon, ma'am. We've looked everywhere, but he's not to be found.'

Mrs Toplady was furious. 'Let me know when he comes in. He's gone to the fair again, I'll be bound. Thomas shall give him a sound thrashing.'

Sam had not appeared when Sarah went up to bed, full of secret fears. And when she ran down next morning there was still no news of him.

She should have been so happy. Today she was going home. But there was a cloud over the house. She must know what had happened to Boy Friday before she left.

Surely he was not hiding in the ice-house? When nobody was about in the yard, she opened the door. No, the candle lay in its usual place just inside. There was only the cold darkness. She called. There was no answer.

Her bag was brought down. Thomas had harnessed her father's horse and their simple country gig stood waiting at the door, so very different from her aunt's grand coach. It was time to say polite goodbyes.

Mrs Toplady could talk of nothing but her wicked chocolate boy. 'He's run away,' she declared. 'But I'll get him back. I'll offer a reward. I'll hunt him to the ends of the earth. He'll be sorry for this.'

At that moment a little group of men came up the street. They looked grim. One of them was carrying a canary-yellow coat. Sarah let out a cry as she saw it.

'Beg pardon, lady,' said the man. 'This was found on the river-bank in the Spa gardens. There's no sign of a body, but it looks as if—'

'The wretched boy has drowned himself!' cried Mrs Toplady in a fury. Sarah burst into tears and everyone began talking at once.

'You – you drove him to it!' she sobbed.

'Hush, Sarah!' begged her father, but he looked even grimmer than the men who had brought the coat.

'I will not have disgraceful scenes outside my own front door,' declared Mrs Toplady.

There seemed nothing to be done but to cut short the farewells and go. Sarah's father helped her gently into the gig, took his seat beside her, and drove off.

Their way took them north across the market-place. It was empty and deserted that morning. All the fair people had packed up early and gone.

Sarah's last view of the town was misted by her tears. She could think of nothing but her poor Boy Friday and his terrible end. Her father tried a few words of comfort, but there was little he could say.

'He must have seen how hopeless it was,' said Sarah. 'If he'd just run away, she'd have hunted him down. As she said.'

'She won't have *that* pleasure now, anyway,' said her father bitterly. 'She knows she's lost him for good.'

They overtook some of the fair people on the road. Some drove waggons loaded with their tents and other gear, others trudged on foot. 'It's a hard life,' he said, 'moving on from town to town. But it's free.'

'Yes,' she said. 'It's free.'

'And they look happy enough.'

At midday they stopped in a small town to rest the horse and eat something themselves at the inn. Farther down the street some of the fair people were setting up their booths. 'They have to earn a penny whenever they can,' he said.

Suddenly Sarah's face lit up. 'Father, listen!'

'You mean that drumming?'

She was off, pattering down the street. He hurried after her. In front, a crowd had already gathered.

It was the same striped tent that she remembered, the same kind-looking, ruddy-cheeked showman in the fancy waistcoat. And beside him, with a look of absolute bliss on his dusky face, Boy Friday was playing the drum.

His eyes met hers. His teeth flashed in the happiest of grins. There was no need for words. There was complete understanding between them.

Half an hour later, Sarah and her father continued their journey home.

'I slipped the lad a guinea,' he said, 'and I had a word with the showman. He seems a decent sort. He'll treat him fairly.' He chuckled. 'And now, dear,

I think we'd better forget that we ever saw him, don't you?'

She knew what he meant. They must never let Mrs Toplady know that her chocolate boy was alive and happy, not drowned at the bottom of the river.

But forget him? Sarah knew that she could never do that.